WORDS
AARON REYNOLDS

PICTURES
PETER BROWN

SIMON & SCHUSTER BOOKS FOR YOUNG READERS
New York   London   Toronto   Sydney   New Delhi

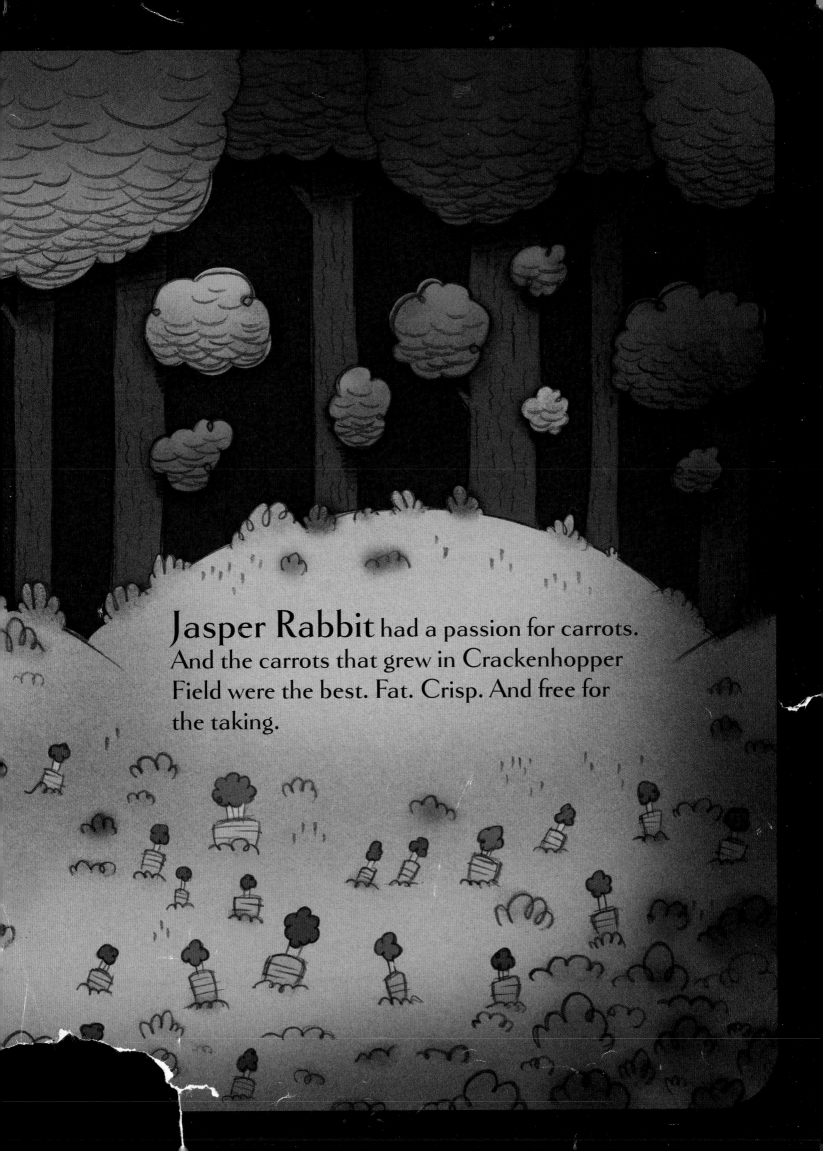

Jasper Rabbit had a passion for carrots.
And the carrots that grew in Crackenhopper
Field were the best. Fat. Crisp. And free for
the taking.

He pulled some for a morning snack on the way to school.

He yanked out a few on his way to Little League practice.

He ripped them from the ground on his way home at night.

Jasper couldn't get enough carrots . . .

. . . until they started following him.

He first noticed something strange after the big game against the East Valley Hares. Jasper was about to help himself to a victory snack . . . when he heard it. The soft . . . sinister . . . *tunktunktunk* of carrots creeping.

He turned . . .

but there was nothing there.

Just my imagination, he thought.
But he hopped a little faster.

That night, as he was brushing his teeth . . .
there they were!

Jasper whipped around . . . but nothing. He laughed at himself, picked his toothbrush off the floor, and went to bed . . . quickly.

The next morning he approached Crackenhopper Field slowly.

He reached for
two wild carrots.
Nothing happened.

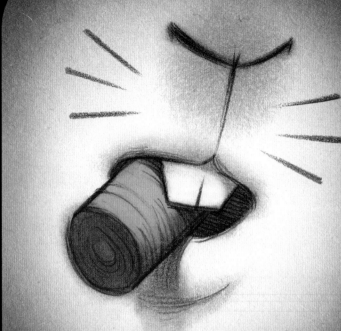

He bit into one.
Nothing happened.

Whew! Creepy carrots . . . It was ridiculous!

But when he arrived home
that evening . . .

"Mom! Mom!" Jasper screamed.
"Creepy carrots! In the shed!"

His mom opened the door slowly. There weren't any carrots.
Not even the regular kind.

"There are no such things as creepy carrots,"
Mom said, shaking her head.

Later that night, as Jasper lay in bed, he heard it.

Breathing.

Terrible, carroty breathing.

And there, on his wall!

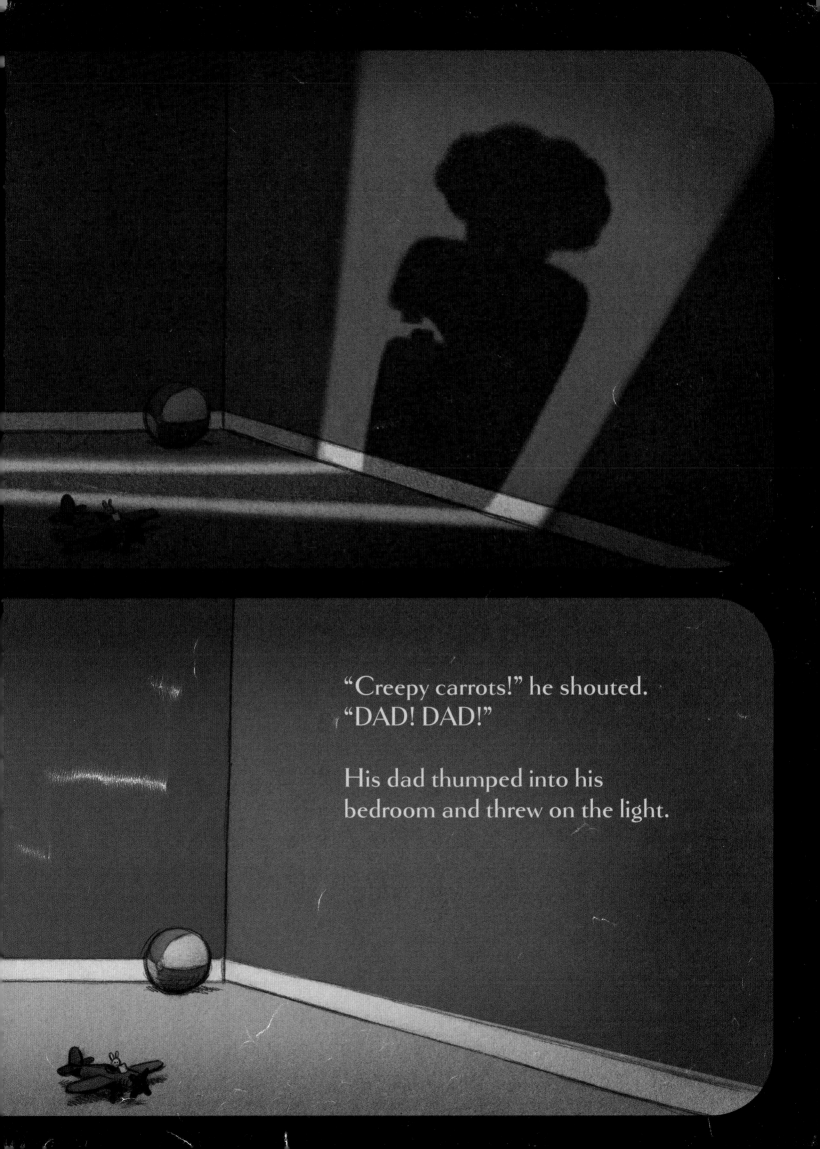

"Creepy carrots!" he shouted.
"DAD! DAD!"

His dad thumped into his
bedroom and threw on the light.

They searched under the bed. No creepy carrots.

They looked through the closet.
No creepy carrots.

They opened the dresser drawers.

No.

Creepy.

Carrots.

"Just a bad dream, son,"
his dad said, shaking his
head. "Now go to sleep."

That wasn't going
to happen.

By the end of the week

Jasper was seeing

creepy carrots creeping

EVERYWHERE.

Jasper knew his parents were wrong. Creepy carrots were real. And they were coming for him!

But they couldn't get him . . .
if they couldn't get out.

Jasper hatched a plan. First thing on Saturday, he grabbed supplies and headed to Crackenhopper Field.

On his way home, there was no *tunktunktunk*.
There were no carrot-shaped shadows. His
plan had worked. No creepy carrots would
ever get out of that carrot patch again.

As the sun finally set across Crackenhopper Field,
Jasper Rabbit smiled.

And as the sun finally set, the carrots of
Crackenhopper Field . . .

cheered!

Their creepy plan had worked.
They were sure of it.

Jasper Rabbit would never get
into that carrot patch ever again.

To Paul Rodeen, a 24-carrot gem of an agent
—A. R.

For Andrew and Kristin
—P. B.

SIMON & SCHUSTER BOOKS FOR YOUNG READERS
An imprint of Simon & Schuster Children's Publishing Division
1230 Avenue of the Americas, New York, New York 10020
Text copyright © 2012 by Aaron Reynolds
Illustrations copyright © 2012 by Peter Brown
SIMON & SCHUSTER BOOKS FOR YOUNG READERS is a trademark of Simon & Schuster, Inc.
For information about special discounts for bulk purchases, please contact
Simon & Schuster Special Sales at 1-866-506-1949 or business@simonandschuster.com.
The Simon & Schuster Speakers Bureau can bring authors to your live event.
For more information or to book an event, contact the Simon & Schuster Speakers Bureau
at 1-866-248-3049 or visit our website at www.simonspeakers.com.
Book design by Lizzy Bromley
The text for this book is set in Goldenbook.
The illustrations for this book are rendered in pencil on paper
and then digitally composited and colored.
Manufactured in China
0914 SCP
14 16 18 20 19 17 15 13
Library of Congress Cataloging-in-Publication Data
Reynolds, Aaron, 1970–
Creepy carrots! / Aaron Reynolds ; illustrated by Peter Brown. — 1st ed.
p. cm.
Summary: The carrots that grow in Crackenhopper Field are the fattest and crispiest around
and Jasper Rabbit cannot resist pulling some to eat each time he passes by, until he begins
hearing and seeing creepy carrots wherever he goes.
ISBN 978-1-4424-0297-3 (hardcover : alk. paper) • ISBN 978-1-4424-5309-8 (eBook)
[1. Carrots—Fiction. 2. Rabbits—Fiction. 3. Humorous stories.] I. Brown, Peter, 1979– ill. II. Title.
PZ7.R33213Cre 2012
[E]—dc22
2010035099